A MESSAGE FROM CHICKEN HOUSE

I've always loved those classic 'bears as best friends' stories, from Pooh to Paddington. It seems to me that animals bring out the best in us and that sometimes we all need a paw to point out what we can do to face up to our problems – as my dog Barbara often shows me! It's the same in Sarah Horne's brilliant *Panda at the Door*, even if the results are hilariously unpredictable . . . This is a glorious, witty and wise new favourite panda for us all!

BARRY CUNNINGHAM
Publisher
Chicken House

PANDA AT THE DOOR

Written by Anna Wilson
with Sarah Horne

2 PALMER STREET, FROME,
SOMERSET BA11 1DS

Illustrations and story © Sarah Horne 2021
From an original idea by Vikki Anderson © The Big Idea Competition Limited 2021
Story written by Anna Wilson with Sarah Horne © Chicken House Publishing Ltd 2021

First published in Great Britain in 2021
Chicken House
2 Palmer Street
Frome, Somerset BA11 1DS
United Kingdom
www.chickenhousebooks.com

Cover design by Helen Crawford-White
Cover and interior illustrations by Sarah Horne
Interior designed and typeset by Steve Wells
Printed and bound in Great Britain by CPI Group (UK) Ltd, Croydon CR0 4YY
The paper used in this Chicken House book is made from wood grown
in sustainable forests.

1 3 5 7 9 10 8 6 4 2

British Library Cataloguing in Publication data available.

ISBN 978-1-911490-01-2
eISBN 978-1-913322-23-6

For Diana

CHAPTER 1
Some UnBEARable News

'I love to laugh! Hahaha!' Pudding hummed to herself after another practically perfect day as the Star Attraction of Edinburgh Zoo. It might not have been obvious to anyone passing that a panda could be an entertainer, but if you stopped and watched, you'd soon agree that Pudding was spectacular at making children smile. 'All. Day. Long!'

she sang, as she waved goodbye to the people who had come to see her. She carried on blowing kisses long after the crowds had disappeared. 'Come back tomorrow!' she called into the chilly evening air. 'It's been lovely having you!'

When it was clear that she was all alone again, Pudding went back into her pen. She sat down with a sigh and turned to her favourite end-of-day pastime: watching the *Mary Poppins* DVD that her keeper, Gerald, had given her when she had first arrived at Edinburgh Zoo as a young cub. He had thought it would make her feel less lonely. And it had.

For a while.

Pudding adored Mary Poppins. She

adored Gerald as well, of course. Both of them, in their different ways, had taught her so much about life. One had taught her how to be polite and cheerful at all times, and the other had taught her how to be a Star Attraction. (One had a a magic umbrella and the other had ginger moustache. No prizes for guessing which was which!)

But neither of them could take the place of a real family.

Pudding sighed again as she watched Mary Poppins fly through the sky with her magic umbrella. 'One day,' she whispered sadly, 'if I practise hard enough, maybe I will be able to fly away like you, Mary Poppins, and find a family to live with. A family who needs me.'

BEEP!

Pudding knew that the beep of Gerald's watch meant bamboo. And sure enough, right on time, here was Gerald with her tea.

'Hullo, Gerald!' Pudding called out. 'Hasn't it been a

supercalifragilisticexpialidocious day?'

'Hmph,' the keeper grunted as he unlocked the panda's pen, struggling under the weight of armfuls of glossy green bamboo shoots. A panda could eat almost her body-weight in leaves every day, so this was something Gerald did often.

'Let me help you with those.' Pudding took the bundles from him.

Gerald mopped his brow. 'Thanks, hen,' he said. 'Och! Ah'm absolutely knackered. Ma flamingos have been givin' me the run-around today.'

'Poor you! What naughty birds,' said Pudding. 'Why don't you sit down and have a rest?'

'Rest!' Gerald grumbled. 'If I sit down, hen, I'll ne'er get up again! I'm no' gettin' any younger – eighty-three next birthday!'

'That *is* very old.' Pudding nodded.

'Thank you very much!' Gerald pretended to be

offended. 'But I'd better no' let the bosses see me sitting down on the job. They're muttering about moving me on as it is.'

Pudding chewed thoughtfully on an especially delicious shoot. 'I suppose I'm not getting any younger either,' she said. She had no idea how old she really was – all she knew was that she had arrived in a crate a long time ago. 'Does *anyone* ever actually get any younger?' she asked, more to herself than to Gerald. 'If that really did happen, I'd be a wee cub and you'd be nothing but a tiny baby.' She chewed some more bamboo. 'I hope the zoo aren't thinking of moving *me* on. Unless . . .' The stalk fell from her mouth as she was struck by a sudden idea. 'Unless it's to find me a family? I should so love to be a nanny with a bag, a hat and an umbrella, just like Mary Poppins. D'you think I'll ever get the chance?'

'Eh?' Gerald wheezed. 'A *nanny*? Who's ever

heard of a nanny *panda*? A nanny *goat*, maybe!' He gave a gruff sort of laugh. 'Yer heid's full o' mince, wee lassie!' Gerald reached over and tickled her behind the ears.

Pudding had no idea what he was talking about. How could someone's head be full of mince? And if goats could be nannies, why couldn't she?

BEEP BEEP!

'Och! This new watch o' mine,' Gerald growled irritably. Pudding peered at the gadget on his wrist. It was very smart – black and shiny with a rectangular face. (Black was Pudding's favourite colour. Her second favourite was white.) The bosses

had given the watch to Gerald for working at the zoo for sixty years – three times a panda's lifetime.

BEEP BEEP BEEP!

'Will you *stop*?' Gerald muttered again.

'Sorry,' said Pudding. 'Did I say something wrong?'

Gerald laughed. 'Not you, soft lass! This bletherin' watch. Sending me messages, telling me how to take care of you, when to feed you – as if ah dinnae ken after sixty years!' He sucked his teeth in annoyance.

'Try not to be cross, Gerald.' Pudding patted his hand. 'It's not good for you.'

'You're a wee sweetie.' He smiled at her. 'Which makes this all the harder to say—'

BEEP BEEP BEEP BEEEEP!

'Gah! Stupid thing!' Gerald cried, tugging his watch off.

'I don't think your watch is listening, Gerald,' Pudding said, trying to be helpful.

BEEEEEEPPP!!

'Grrrr!' Gerald's eyebrows became one long caterpillar frown. He stuffed the watch carelessly into his pocket.

'Why don't you just read whatever it's telling you, Gerald? It might be an important message,' Pudding said.

'It's nothin'...' Gerald faltered. 'Now, how about you tuck into your tea and I'll get you some clean fresh bedding?'

Pudding knew that in spite of Gerald's complaints, his watch had proved useful from time to time. There had been that incident with Larry, the blue-bottomed baboon, for example, who had stowed away with a man in a van. Thanks to the tracking device on Larry's right foot, and the 'Find My Ape' app on Gerald's watch, the keeper had been first on the scene.

Pudding shook her head. Humans could be such dafties. Anyway, whatever the zoo was worried about, that was Gerald's problem. Pudding had a show to practise – and, as everyone knows, *practice makes practically perfect.*

'Tomorrow, Gerald, will be my BEST,' she raised a paw above her head, 'my most EXCITING,' she turned her feet to three o'clock, 'most WONDER-FUL,' she looked skywards and hitched up an imaginary skirt, 'Panda Show EVER!'

'That's right, lass,' Gerald mumbled. He hung his head. 'You make it yer best show, because it may be yer last.'

Pudding stopped in mid-dance and stared at him. 'I beg your pardon. What do you mean?'

BEEEP! BEEEP! BEEEEP!

'Och, PIPE DOWN!'

'I can see you're upset, Gerald, but there's really no need to be rude.' Her keeper was behaving very strangely, Pudding thought.

'I wisnae shouting at you, hen. It's ma watch – and those bossy bosses trying tae tell me ma job!' He was gabbling now. 'If they had let me set up the adoption scheme sooner, I could have saved you instead of sending you away—' Gerald stopped abruptly. 'Aaagh! Did I just say that out loud?'

'Adoption? Saved me? *Sending me away?*' Pudding echoed.

＞ ‖ ＜

Gerald's face went bright red. He had the look of a strangled ostrich.

'Gerald? Sending me away? *Where?*' Pudding demanded.

Gerald shuffled his feet. 'We-ell . . .' he said.

'Well, *what*, Gerald?' Pudding insisted.

Gerald cleared his throat. 'You know that it's not possible for you to be a nanny, don't you, Pud?' He patted her shoulder. 'You're a panda. A bear. You cannae live with a human family.'

'Why ever not?' Pudding asked with a small but fierce frown.

Gerald shook his head. 'It breaks ma heart to tell you.' He had tears in his eyes. 'You're a wee panda, darlin',' he said, 'rare and wild. But that's all you'll ever be. And pandas need to have cubs so there are more pandas in this world. Where would we be without bairns?'

'What are you saying, Gerald?' Pudding tried a growl, hoping it would persuade her keeper to answer her properly.

'The management – the bosses,' Gerald muttered, glancing around as if there might be spies listening in. 'They're sending you to . . .' he dropped his voice a notch lower, *'China.'*

Pudding's jaw dropped. 'China? Where's that?' She'd heard of china plates and china teapots, but she had never heard of a *place* called China. 'I don't understand. Have I done something wrong? I—'

Gerald took her paw. 'It's nothin' you've done,' he said,

sighing. 'It's the way o' things. I'm sorry, I really am. More than I can say.'

Poor Gerald, Pudding thought. He looked so sad.

'Ah'm gonna miss you so much, lass,' he continued. 'But there's nothin' I can do. I'm an auld man and no one listens to me.' He let go of her paw. 'Bye-bye, hen,' he said. 'I'll see you in the mornin'. One last time. Who knows, maybe the wind will change and bring better things our way?'

And with that, Gerald turned and walked out.

Pudding sat hunched on the cold concrete floor. Not even a bottom as plump and furry as hers could soften the chill that was running through her. How long had Gerald known about a plan to send her away? How many times had he come to feed her since he'd known – and he had said NOTHING?

As if in reply, there was a muffled sound from underneath the stack of newspapers that was her bed.

Gerald's watch! It must have fallen from his pocket.

Pudding rummaged around and found it. *I'll see*

what those messages say for myself, she thought. *Perhaps it was all a silly mistake? After all, Mary Poppins always says you should never judge things by their appearance.* But as she read and re-read the messages, finally she had to accept it: it wasn't a mistake. It was true. All of it. Every single last word.

Well, I won't go! she fumed to herself. *They can't make me. I'll run away first!*

BEEP! The watch pinged again. Pudding stared at the tiny screen. It was blinking to say that there was a new message, but this one wasn't from any horrible bosses — it was from someone called Callum Campbell.

Dear Pudding. I don't

know why I am writing this. But whatever, I need your help . . .

Pudding blinked and rubbed her eyes. She couldn't believe it! *A message for me – from a child in need?* It was as if Mary Poppins had answered her most heartfelt wish! She closed her eyes and clasped her paws to her big warm heart, feeling it skip a beat. A child had come to her rescue. They could rescue *each other!*

All she had to do was escape.

But *how*? She'd never tried escaping before. Pudding opened her eyes and went over to her barred door. 'Grrrr!' She tried to pull the bars apart, but they refused to budge. Then she blinked again, this time in amazement, as the door swung open all by itself.

'Oh!' Pudding cried. 'Gerald, my dear friend – you've set me free!'

Out she crept into the night, and a strange breeze filled the trees as she took her first steps out into the city to find the boy who needed her.

Who knows, she thought, *maybe the wind really is changing . . .*

CHAPTER 2
A Very Un-Birthday Day

Earlier that same day, on the other side of the city, Callum Campbell was on his way back from school. It was his birthday – his ninth birthday. He should have been running home to a cake and piles of presents. Instead, he was dragging his feet and staring at the ground as he trudged up the hill towards home. The wind was getting up, and he shivered as he pulled his coat around him.

'I don't feel *nine*,' he muttered to himself. 'I don't even feel birthday-ish.' Today just felt like yesterday, and the day before that – a wet-sock, cold-custard, squashed-fly sort of day.

THUD!

Something hit Cal hard on the back of the legs. He wheeled around – it was a football. He looked up to see Mike Spiker from across the street standing there, laughing at him.

'Ha! Check your face!' the boy jeered. 'Never were any good at footie, were ye?'

'Go 'way, Spiker,' Cal said. He went to walk away, but Spiker blocked him, dribbling the football in front of him. Cal tried to move past, first to the left, then to the right, but Spiker always

got there first. This was typical of him – he was the meanest kid in Cal's class. Spiker by name, spiky by nature. And always out to make Cal's life difficult.

'Gi's yer money, birthday boy, and I'll leave ye alone,' said Spiker.

'Haven't got any,' Cal replied. Hot tears pricked at his eyes.

'Och, that's right,' Spiker sneered. 'I forgot. You gave me yer dinner money already, didn't ye?' He took a step back and swung at the ball, kicking it straight into Cal's stomach and sending him reeling. Then he scooped the ball up and ran off with it, laughing.

Cal picked himself up from the cold cobblestones. *I did so not 'give' you anything, Mike Spiker,* he said to himself. *I'll 'give' you a football in the face next time I see you, though.*

He sighed. How come he always thought of clever things to say *after* Spiker had been

horrible to him? He looked up at Arthur's Seat and imagined what it would be like to be a king whom everyone feared and obeyed. *I'd like to see the look on Mike Spiker's face if King Arthur demanded he hand over his dinner money,* he thought.

At that moment the low winter sun lit up the top of the hill in a crown of golden rays. Perhaps King Arthur was sending him a message: 'It'll be all right. Just you wait and see.' The thought cheered Cal up. *Maybe things will be all right. Maybe Mum and Dad have stopped arguing. Maybe they're waiting for me at home with big cheesy grins on their faces and a pile of pressies!*

The idea sent Cal sprinting up his street. He ran to his front door, fumbled with his key in the lock, then threw himself into the hall, shouting, 'It's me! I'm home!' He could hear muffled voices in the kitchen. This was it. Any minute now they'd jump out and surprise him—

'Look, you *know* things've been tough lately...' he heard Dad saying.

'Call your-self a comedian? You're not making

me laugh any more . . .' Mum's voice was shrill.

Cal skidded to a halt in the hall. His parents were fighting. Again. And on his birthday. How could they?

The hot tears that had pricked at his eyes earlier finally started to spill down his face. Cal brushed them away angrily. *Some birthday!* He stood in the hallway, his hands over his ears. He wished he could go to Neil's, but his best pal had moved away a few months back. It wasn't fair. Nothing was fair.

Even with his ears covered, he could still hear his parents arguing.

'You need to start bringing home the bacon – same as me!' Mum was saying angrily.

'*Me* bring home the bacon?' Cal heard his dad shout back. 'Why can't you *save* our bacon for once instead of throwing good bacon after bad?'

'That's it!' Cal muttered. He marched towards

the kitchen door. 'Arguing about bacon! How stupid is that?'

Just then, Dad stormed out into the hallway.

'Dad?' Cal said.

'Don't you dare walk away from me, Graham!' Cal's mum shouted after him.

Dad didn't reply. He walked right past Cal without seeing him and grabbed a coat from the pegs on the wall. Then, with his head down, he pushed open the front door and stomped out into the fading evening light, leaving the door to slam shut behind him.

'Dad!' Cal shouted, running out after him into

the street. But Dad's long legs had already carried him off into the shadows.

Cal stopped. There was no use chasing after him. 'DAD!' he shouted one last time, his voice so high and reedy that the wind whistled it away.

'Shouting for Daddy like a wee bairn, are we?' Cal didn't have to turn to know it was Spiker again. 'Left you at last, has he?' Spiker jeered from across the street. 'I don't blame him. Bet he's fed up o' having a squirt like you for a son.'

'Shut up, Spiker,' Cal growled. 'He hasn't left us. He's just . . . gone to get some bacon,' he said, thinking on his feet. Well, that was what Mum and

Dad had been fighting about, anyway.

Spiker sniggered again. 'My dad says your dad is a massive waste of space. A *clown*, isn't he? Like, who has an actual clown for a dad?'

Cal felt a red-hot rush of anger. He made his hands into tight fists. 'My dad is *not* a clown!' he shouted. 'He is a stand-up comedian!'

Spiker took a hasty step back – he wasn't used to Cal acting tough. 'Whatever,' he snapped. 'My dad says no one thinks he's funny, not even your mum—'

'MIKEY!' someone yelled from inside the Spikers' house. 'GET IN HERE, NOW!'

Spiker froze and glanced over his shoulder. A burly figure was swaggering towards them: Spud Spiker, Mike's dad.

'I told ye I wanted ye home to cook ma tea!' Spiker's dad yelled. 'Wha' ye doin' bletherin' out here with that idiot?' he added, glaring at Cal.

Spiker's eyes were wide with fear. 'Sorry, Dad! Comin', Dad!' he spluttered. Then he wheeled around back to Cal and said menacingly, 'I'll see *you* later, Callum Campbell,' before running off home.

Cal let out a long low breath. *That was close,* he thought. *My birthday nearly got a whole lot worse.*

He turned and went back into his house and shut the door behind him. It was deathly quiet inside now. *Maybe this is just another of Dad's practical jokes?* Dad was dead good at practical jokes. Cal remembered when Dad had put salt in the sugar bowl and Mum and Tabby had sprinkled it on their cornflakes. *Maybe they've all run into the lounge to hide behind the sofa, ready to jump out and shout, 'Gotcha!'?*

Maybe he was a wally to even think so.

Cal tiptoed into the lounge. There was no one there, but as he took in the empty room, Cal spotted something that he hadn't noticed this morning. On the mantelpiece was an envelope – a big brown one with Cal's name on. His spirits lifted at the sight of it.

Too big to be a card, he thought. *Maybe there's some money inside? Or a voucher to a theme park! Or the climbing arena? Something cool like that.*

He reached up. His fingers were about to touch the envelope when he felt a sharp poke in his back.

'Oi!' he cried, whipping around. Too late – his little sister, Tabby, had snatched the envelope from under his nose.

'Gimme that!' Cal yelled.

'Shan't. Finders keepers. It's MINE now,' Tabby said. She danced away from him and held the envelope out in front of her, whisking it back again as her brother darted towards her.

'Give it back!' Cal said. 'That's MY name on the front!'

'Want it? Can't haaaave it!' Tabby sang, jumping on to the sofa and dangling the envelope just out of Cal's reach.

Cal flung himself at her and they went tumbling on to the floor in a squabbling ball, knocking over lamps and sending cushions flying.

'MUMMY!' Tabby wailed.

Mrs Campbell came running into the room. Her

face was smeary and crumpled, as if she had been crying too. 'What on earth is going on here, Callum? What've you done to your sister?'

'*She* started it!' Cal protested.

Mrs Campbell glared at him as she picked Tabby up and kissed her wet pink cheek. '*Really?* I don't think so – she's only six,' she said, looking at the mess that surrounded her.

'But she—'

'Listen, I've got enough to worry about – I mean, with your dad . . . oh, it doesn't matter. Just get changed out of your uniform, Cal. OK?'

More angry tears threatened to spill from Cal's eyes.

'Callum's a crybaby!' Tabby sang under her breath.

'Tabitha!' Mum said in a warning tone.

'He's just sad, Mummy, 'cause it's his birthday and you've forgotten,' Tabby blurted out.

'OH NO!' Mum gasped, her hands flying to her mouth. She looked so upset that Cal wanted to tell her it didn't matter. He didn't care about his stupid birthday anyway – he just wanted Dad back, and for him and Mum to stop fighting.

'Look – sweetheart, we hadn't forgotten,' Mum gabbled. She rescued the envelope from Tabby. 'See what we got you? You open it, while I get the tea on. Come on, Tabs. You can help me.'

Mum rushed off to the kitchen, leaving Cal to

slowly turn the envelope over. It was bent in the corner where Tabby had clutched it. It didn't look very special – more like a school report or something. He tore it open, and out fell a Certificate of Adoption from Edinburgh Zoo with a panda printed on it.

hello!

Thank you for adopting me!

MY NAME IS PUDDING THE PANDA BEAR. I AM THE STAR ATTRACTION AT EDINBURGH ZOO! YOU CAN COME VISIT ME FOR FREE ANYTIME BY SHOWING THIS CARD AT THE ENTRANCE.
YOU CAN ALSO <u>EMAIL ME</u>: puddingpanda @edinburghzoo.com
ASK ME ANYTHING!
+ SEE YOU SOON. XOXO ♥

Cal's heart sank into his school socks as he read on.

'Nooo!'

This was the last straw. Cal finally boiled over.

'This isn't a proper present. THIS IS RUBBISH!' he shouted, loud enough for Mum to hear. Then he ran upstairs and threw himself on to his bed. This was the worst-est birthday ever!

Some time later, Cal emerged from under his duvet. He had fallen asleep fully clothed. It was dark outside now, and an owl was hooting. A shaft of moonlight caught the edge of the adoption certificate, which lay on the floor where it had landed.

Cal picked it up and leant over to turn on his bedside lamp. He read the words aloud.

'You can also email me:

at puddingpanda@edinburghzoo.com. Ask me anything!'

He scowled. 'Huh. OK, answer this one, then, Pudding the Panda!'

He jumped up to get his tablet from his desk. *Dear Pudding.* His fingers stabbed at the keyboard as he typed.

To: PUDDINGPANDA@EDINBURGHZOO.COM
Subject: YOUR CARD IS RUBBISH!

DEAR PUDDING,

I DON'T KNOW WHY I AM WRITING THIS. BUT WHATEVER, I NEED YOUR HELP. MY NAME IS CALLUM CAMPBELL AND "APPARENTLY" I ADOPTED YOU. I AM 9 YEARS OLD TODAY. MY DAD ISN'T HERE, MY SISTER TABBY IS THE MOST ANNOYING PERSON ON THE PLANET, MY BEST PAL NEIL McGREGOR HAS MOVED AWAY. I AM BEING BULLIED BY MIKE SPIKER AND MY MUM IS SO UPSET WITH MY DAD. SHE FORGOT MY BIRTHDAY TODAY. MY QUESTION FOR YOU IS WHEN WILL I BE HAPPY AGAIN? (HELP WITH THAT ONE IF YOU CAN!) HAHAHA. AS IF. AND TELL NEIL TO COME AND VISIT. neilmcg@yalloo.com

YOURS MISERABLY,
CALLUM CAMPBELL

42, BUMBLESCRAPE STREET
EDINBURGH, SCOTLAND,
EUROPE, THE WORLD,
THE UNIVERSE.

Cal pressed SEND and watched as his message was sucked into cyberspace. Then he shook his head. What was he even thinking – writing to a panda? He slumped back on to his bed and stared out of the window, listening to the wind. It was a stormy night out there.

Where's Dad? I hope he's somewhere safe in all that wind. Maybe if I wish him home hard enough, he'll be back here in the morning.

Cal squeezed his eyes shut. He tried to picture his dad waiting for him in the kitchen at breakfast, all smiles and jokes and back to his funny old self. Soon the images in his head became jumbled. Dad vanished, and instead there was a black-and-white bear sitting at the table . . .

Cal had fallen asleep again.

DING DONG!

'What the—?' Cal leapt out of bed. The front

doorbell was ringing.

He ran out on to the landing and squinted into the early-morning sunlight that streamed through the windows. Tabby was already up and shouting, 'Dad! It's Dad! Wake up, everyone! He's come back!'

That was enough to send Cal pushing past his little sister and rocketing down the stairs.

'DA!' he yelled, launching himself at the front door.

DING DONG!

DING DONG!

'All right, Graham. We're coming!' As it was a Saturday, Mum was still in her PJs and bed socks. 'Why haven't you got your keys?'

DING DONG! DING DONG! DING DONG! DING DONG!

Cal gave the doorknob a big tug. And there, on the top step, stood . . .

'Good morning,' said the bear, extending her paw politely. 'I'm Pudding the Panda, here to help. May I come in?'

'WHOA!' Cal cried, backing away from the panda in shock.

'Mum! Mum!' Tabby screamed from behind him. 'Mum! There's a . . . there's a PANDA AT THE DOOR!'

Mum's eyes opened wide. They opened so wide that her eyeballs rolled up into the back of her head. Then, letting out a long breathy *ahhhh,* she fell to the floor in a dead faint.

CHAPTER 3
Panda to the Rescue!

'Oh no! The poor woman!' the panda exclaimed. 'Quick, children. A spoonful of sugar for the shock. Spit spot!'

Tabby and Cal shuffled to one side like sleep-walkers and let the bear in. Cal was still blinking and pinching himself. *I'm still asleep*, he thought. *I'm dreaming. I must be.*

'Ooh,' whispered Tabby. She nudged Cal. 'It must be a panda from the zoo!'

Cal couldn't speak. *So, I'm not dreaming, then?* he thought. *Tabby can see it too?*

Tabby, on the other hand, had a million and one questions for the bear. 'Pudding? That's a funny name. How did you find us? Why did the zoo let you out? Was that a flamingo flying away just then? And what's Mum's flowerpot doing on your head?'

Cal took another look at the panda. Tabby was quite right – it was wearing Mum's flowerpot as a hat! Not only that, but Mum's precious pansies were scattered on the floor, along with a wriggling worm and quite a lot of earth. *Mum's not going to like that!* Cal thought.

'It's lovely to meet you, child, but we must help your poor mummy first,' the bear said to Tabby.

'Sugar. A spoonful. Hurry!'

'I'll get it!' Tabby ran off into the kitchen.

Cal finally found his voice. 'You – you – you can't just burst into our house like this!' he protested.

'Well, if I'm not needed here, then I must have got the wrong address,' said the panda. She put Mum gently into a more comfortable position, then checked a shiny black watch that encircled her paw. 'This *is* 42 Bumblescrape Street, isn't it? And this email is from—'

'Wait!' said Cal. 'You got my email? For *real*?'

'If you're Callum Campbell, then yes, I did. And in the nick of time, it seems.'

Tabby had come back with the sugar. She had spilt most of it, but she handed the spoon proudly to the panda anyway. 'Are you here to stay?' she asked. 'You can sleep in my room if you like.'

Pudding gave a chuckle. 'I don't think nannies

sleep in the same room as their charges,' she said. 'In any case, it was Callum who sent for me. It seems I was his birthday present.'

Tabby crossed her arms. Her face was thunderous. Cal knew what was coming next.

'How come *Cal* gets the best birthday present in the world?' she demanded. 'Why didn't *I* get a panda on MY birthday?'

'Keep your voice down,' Cal shushed her. 'Poor Mum. She's going to get an even bigger shock when she wakes up. And she's having a bad enough time as it is, what with Dad . . .'

'You told me about that in your message.' The panda sat down on the floor next to Mum. She patted a space beside her. There wasn't much room, and Cal felt the wooden floorboards creak with her weight as she shuffled up to make space. 'You asked me to help, Callum, so here I am.'

'Cooool!' Tabby climbed fearlessly into Pudding's lap. She reached up and touched the flowerpot on the panda's head. 'That IS Mum's flowerpot, isn't it?'

'I like to look the part,' said Pudding, dusting off some ants from her shoulders.

'Part of what?' asked Cal suspiciously.

Pudding looked astounded. 'Why, the part of nanny,' she repeated. 'You know – like Mary Poppins, who comes to look after unhappy children?'

Cal looked at her blankly.

Pudding made an exasperated noise. 'I've come to play the part of nanny to the *unhappy boy who wrote to me last night*,' she said, eyeing Cal meaningfully.

'What, me?' Cal said.

Pudding nodded.

'But I don't need a nanny!' Cal protested. 'Nannies are for babies. If you're going to stay here, you can be Tabby's nanny.' He felt all hot and bothered – he wished he hadn't sent that email. He hadn't expected anyone to answer it – let alone a bear.

'Hey, I am *not* a baby!' Tabby objected.

'Shut up, Tabs. Listen, Pudding – if that's really your name –' Cal stood up and spoke firmly – 'you can't stay here, all right?'

'So why did you message me, then? Look – I'll read out what you wrote.' She tapped at the black watch she was wearing and read aloud: '*My name is Callum Campbell and "apparently" I adopted you. I am 9 years old today. My dad isn't here, my sister Tabby is the most annoying person on the planet—*'

'HEY!' Tabby shouted at Cal. 'I am NOT annoying.'

'Shut up, Tabs!' Cal gave her a shove. 'You're being annoying right now.'

'AM NOT!'

'That's enough, both of you,' said Pudding. Then she took hold of Tabby's collar in one paw, and Cal's in the other, and lifted them both clean off the ground.

'HEY!' they cried in unison.

'Wh-wh-what's going on?' Mum said. She had come out of her faint and was looking very dazed. 'Graham?' She peered up at the panda. 'Is that you in there? Why are you dressed as a bear?'

Pudding put the children down and bent to take Mum's hand. She stroked it gently. 'There, there, Mrs Campbell,' she said. 'I'm here to help you too.' She straightened her flowerpot hat. 'But my name's not Graham, it's Pudding. I'm your new nanny. I make the impossible possible! Now,

how about a spoonful of sugar for the shock?' She
reached for the spoon beside her.

Mum's eyes widened once more.

'Don't faint again, Mum!' Cal cried.

But his mum wasn't going to crumple this time. She was staring in disbelief at Pudding's soft paw, offering her a spoonful of sugar. She took the spoon away and turned the paw over in her hand. She examined the panda's claws one by one. Then she let the paw drop and got up and walked around the panda, checking her all over as though looking for something lost in the bear's fur. 'Graham? This isn't one of your jokes, now?' she asked.

Pudding frowned. 'I told you. I'm not Graham.'

Mum prodded the panda and inspected her fur. 'No poppers . . . no zips . . . no fasteners . . . well!' Mum stopped pacing and shook her head again. 'Perhaps you *are* a panda.' She blinked hard. 'Yup, you're still there,' she said in wonder.

'Mum, we can see it too,' said Cal. 'It *is* a panda. You're not dreaming.'

'Yes!' said Tabby, jumping up and down. 'It's a

real, live panda, and it's come to live with us!'

'With *me*,' Cal corrected her. 'It's *my* birthday present.' He didn't want a nanny, but he wasn't going to let his sister win an argument.

Tabby gave a gasp of outrage. 'Mum! Cal won't share the panda!'

Pudding picked Tabby up again and looked her straight in the eye. 'I am sure we can all learn to share,' she said firmly. Then, setting Tabby down, she turned to Cal and said, 'But please – I'm a *she*, not an it.'

Mum smiled feebly at that. 'I don't mind who or what you are. I don't even mind if I'm seeing things. If you can stop these two from fighting then you're hired!'

Tabby cheered and clapped her hands. 'Yippeeee!'

But Cal was not so easily won over. 'I do NOT need a nanny, Mum,' he said. 'Plus, she's *a bear!* Who ever heard of a panda as a nanny?'

Mum shrugged. 'People let you down, pet. With your dad gone, I'll need some help, so why not a panda? Now, I'm going to have a shower before breakfast.

It's still early.' And with that, she turned and went back upstairs, still wearing a dazed expression.

'*Breakfast!*' said Pudding to Cal. 'I thought you'd never ask – I'm famished. A panda eats almost her body-weight in food every day, you know!'

'Wow, that's a lot of toast!' Cal muttered. 'But I think what Mum really means is, can you help us to make breakfast?'

'We could make PANCAKES!' said Tabby, taking hold of Pudding's paw as if she never wanted to never let go of it.

'Panda cakes?' said Pudding. She scratched her chin. 'I was rather hoping for bamboo, but if you say you have cakes for pandas, that sounds practically perfect! A day-late birthday breakfast for Callum. Better late than never at all!' She gave the children a wink. 'Well, don't just stand there staring, Callum Campbell. Best paw forward!' Leaning down to Tabby, she murmured, 'So how do we make panda cakes?'

'I don't know, I'm only six.' Tabby giggled and tugged Pudding by the paw, leading her into the kitchen.

Cal had no choice but to act fast. If he didn't, Tabby would be sure to take over. And if Pudding really was his birthday present, he was not going to allow that to happen!

'It's PANcakes, not panda cakes. I'll get the recipe.'

He elbowed his way past Tabby. Part of his brain was still saying, *What are you doing? This isn't real, you know!* But he shoved the thought aside. A panda at the door was better than a crying Mum – and a missing Dad.

At this moment, it really did seem as though the impossible had become possible.

CHAPTER 4
Panda-cakes!

Cal rummaged through the kitchen bookshelf and found a recipe for pancakes. He got out the ingredients and the utensils they would need. Then he called out the instructions in his best teacher's voice. 'Crack two eggs in a bowl!'

SMASH! went Tabby.

'Now add the flour!'

WHUMP! went an entire bagful.

'Then the milk, and whisk carefully!'

Pudding scratched her head. 'That's odd,' she said. 'When Mary Poppins clicks her fingers – *spit spot* – everything goes where it's supposed to go.'

When she tried it, the result was not the same at all. It was more . . . lots of spots and splats.

'STOP!' Cal shouted, throwing his hands up in horror at the mess.

'What's wrong?' Pudding asked. 'Don't you like panda cakes?'

'For the last time, it's *pancakes*, not panda cakes!' said Cal crossly. 'And we're going to have to clean up all this before Mum sees. I don't want her upset again.'

'Grumpy-pants!'
Tabby shouted, stirring
her bowl like a wild thing. She was so covered in
batter that Cal could have made her into a pancake.

'Tabby, dear, don't be unkind,' said Pudding. 'And
Callum – try to find the fun!'

'There's nothing fun about tidying
up.' Cal scowled.

Tabby stuck out her tongue.
'Grumpy-pants – with ants!'

'That's enough, both of you,' said
the panda. 'Find the fun when there is a
job to be done, then every task becomes . . . easy
squeezy!' She picked up a lemon and crushed
it into the mixture – peel, pips and all.

'Look, it's nice of you to come here
and help us, but now it's time for
you to go,' Cal said firmly.

Tabby flicked her spoon, and a blob of pancakey goo landed on Cal's cheek. 'You are mean and boring! Pudding is your special birthday present from Mum and Dad. You should be happy. Who else gets a bear to make them breakfast?'

At the mention of Dad, Cal felt sick. In the excitement of Pudding's arrival, he had almost managed to forget about Dad walking out. Now all his worries came surging back. Why hadn't Dad come home yet?

Pudding saw Cal's face fall. She took off her flowerpot hat and reached out a paw. 'Come here,' she said, and she pulled Cal into a bear hug big enough to make his eyes water. At first he tried to wriggle free, but Pudding was so warm and solid and comforting that soon it was easier to give up the struggle and simply sink into all that lovely soft fur. Cal sighed. It was like being wrapped up in a warm towel after a cold swim.

'My poor sad boy!' Pudding patted his head. 'Don't you worry. We'll have this place spit-spolished in two toots of a bagpipe – and then I'll deal with the problem of your parents.'

An hour later, Mum came back downstairs. She stood in the kitchen doorway and blinked at the scene before her.

'Wow!' she said. 'I went back to bed and told myself I must have dreamt about a panda turning up on the doorstep. But it's true! You're here, our very own nanny panda – or, should I say, au pair bear!' She laughed as she took in the now-squeaky-clean surfaces and wiped-down walls. 'Pudding, you really are *perfectly practical* in every way!'

Mum and Pudding were soon gossiping like old friends. Mum looked like the smiley Mum he knew, who would never forget a birthday.

They chatted for a long time. Tabby had quietened down. She had climbed on to Pudding's knee, and although she still had sugar in her ears, she was being more well-behaved than she had been in months.

Cal watched as Pudding listened carefully to everything Mum told her, from Dad going missing through to forgetting Cal's birthday. It occurred to Cal that if anyone walked in, they would think they were one, normal happy family having a relaxed Saturday morning together – if you ignored the fact that there was a panda at the table, that is. *The only thing missing is Dad,* Cal thought.

DING DONG! DING DONG! DING DONG! It was the front doorbell again. Mum, Tabby and Cal glanced at each other.

'I'll get it. It's got to be Dad this time!' Cal ran into the hall and wrenched the front door open.

But it wasn't. It was his best pal, Neil, standing on the top step with a birthday gift in his hands. Mum came up behind Cal and put a hand on his shoulder.

'Oh, Neil! It's you! Lovely to see you, pet,' she said. Cal could tell that, like him, she was doing her

best to sound happy to see his friend, instead of disappointed not to see Dad. 'Ah, well, I'll be in the kitchen,' she said softly. 'I'm going to make some calls to see if I can find – well, you know . . .' And she left Cal to it.

'Hey, Cal. I – I'm sorry I didn't call yesterday,' Neil stammered. 'But when I got your message this morning, I made Mum bring me over.'

Cal's mind went blank. *What message?*

Then he remembered – his email! He had put Neil's email address at the bottom of the note he had sent to Pudding. He gulped. Had she contacted Neil? And where was the bear right now? How could he ever explain what a real panda was doing here!

Neil, meanwhile, was nudging him with the present he'd brought. 'Are you going to let me in then, Cal?' he said. 'Here you go. Better late than—'

'Er, no, *no*, you can't come in,' Cal began awkwardly. 'I'm sorry . . .'

'Oh, yes, he can!' said a bear-y deep voice from behind him.

The colour drained from Neil's face as he pointed a shaking finger past Cal at Pudding.

'P-p-anda . . . !' he stammered.

Cal glanced back, gesturing with his head for Pudding to go away. But the panda stayed right where she was. Thinking fast, Cal turned back to Neil. 'Hahaha! Gotcha! It's only Dad!' he lied. 'He's got a new act.'

It was the worst whopper of his life. Cal felt bad. He hated fibbing to his best pal – especially when he hadn't seen him for so long. But how could he tell him what was really going on? There was nothing for it – Neil would have to leave. Cal began steering his friend gently back the way he had come in. 'It's been great to see you, but we're a wee bit busy right now . . .'

But Cal had not reckoned on Pudding.

'How rude, Callum Campbell!' The panda waggled a claw. 'You told me you wanted to see Neil, so why turn him away now? We've even made panda cakes – I mean, pancakes!'

Neil was opening and closing his mouth like a fish out of water. 'It – it speaks!' he gasped.

"Course it does,' said Cal, chewing his lip. 'Because

it's Dad – I told you.'

'But that outfit is so realistic,' said Neil, pushing past Cal. He walked up to Pudding, inspecting her from every angle, just as Mum had done. He even prodded her backside. Pudding gave an indignant wiggle that almost sent Neil flying.

'Well! I think that's enough of that, young man!' said the panda, stepping back and rubbing her bottom. 'I'll leave you two boys to catch up, then, shall I?' she added, with a bear-glare at Neil. 'I'll be in the kitchen with your mum and Tabby, Callum.'

'Hey, your dad's *really* good!' Neil whispered.

'Yeah, the best,' Cal murmured with relief, dragging his friend off to the lounge and shutting the door firmly behind them. 'And Pud— I mean, Dad's right, Neil – please stay.'

Now that it was just him and his pal – and a cool-looking present – the knot of worry in Cal's tummy was beginning to loosen at last. He slid to the floor in relief and looked at the present on his lap. 'Shall I open it?'

"Course,' said Neil, sliding down next to him.

Cal ripped into the wrapping paper. 'Oh, wow! Lego Marvel Super Heroes? No way, that's brilliant! Thanks, Neil, you're the best!'

Neil blushed. 'I know you've wanted them for ages,' he said. 'Shall we set them up now?'

Soon the two friends were concentrating so hard on the Lego that neither of them saw the sneaky face peering in through the living-room window. But the face had seen them – and a whole lot more besides.

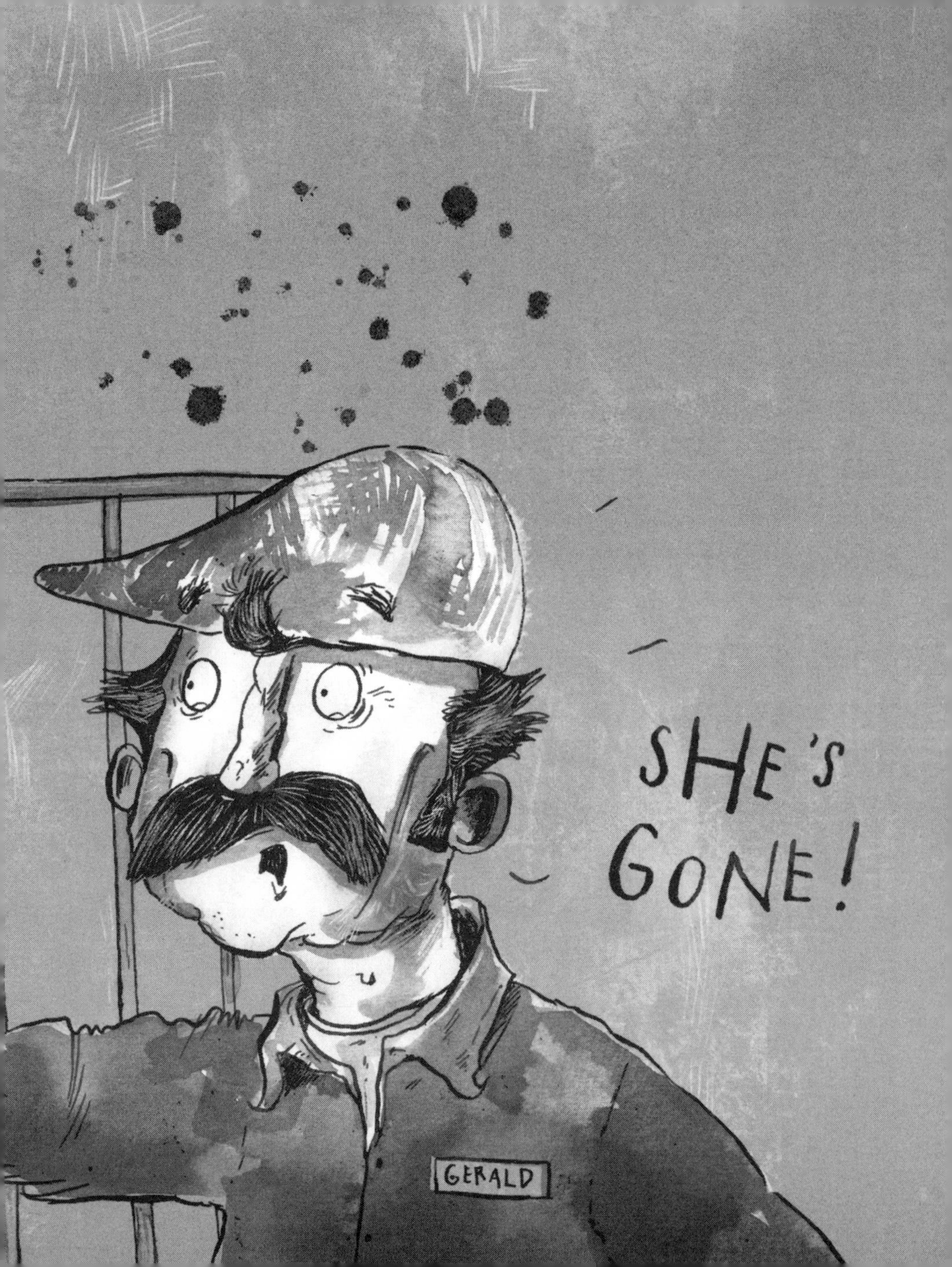
SHE'S GONE!
GERALD

CHAPTER 5

Panda-monium!

That same morning, Gerald had gone to feed Pudding earlier than usual. He made his way to her pen with a heavy heart: this would be the last morning he would ever spend with her. How on earth was he going to find the words to say goodbye? How would he tell her how much he was going to miss her?

He was stopped in his tracks by the sight that greeted him. He stared, shook his head and stared some more. No, no, NO! Pudding's door was wide open, and there was no sign of the panda.

'Sweet heavenly haggis!' Gerald dropped the bamboo he was carrying and ran into the pen. 'Pudding?' he called. 'PUDDING?'

Her bed had not been slept in. Gerald searched high and low, in every nook and cranny, but there

was no avoiding it: the panda had gone.

He ran out into the zoo. He looked left, then right. He looked up, he looked down. She wasn't up to mischief with Larry, the troublesome blue-bottomed baboon. Or chatting with Minnie and the other meerkats. Or playing with the turtles, Dot and Dash. Or bothering Bob the sloth. She wasn't even paddling with her best friends Flop, Flap and Swoop, the flamingos.

Gerald went back to Pudding's empty pen. He mopped his brow. 'How in the name of Nessie will

I find her now?' he said aloud. There was nothing else for it. He'd have to tell the bosses. 'Och, no!' he muttered, as he looked at his watch and realized it wasn't there. 'I've only gone an' lost ma watch as well!'

Cal and Neil were having fun. It was as if his best pal had never moved away. The two of them had spent ages setting up the Lego, and Cal was now laughing at Neil's stories about the kids at his new school. Neil could do impressions of them all.

'Oh, and there's this one lad called Gary,' Neil was saying. 'Gary the Gorilla, they should call him.' He jumped up and began swinging his arms and lumbering about in a gorilla-style walk. 'Uh-uh-uh,' he grunted. 'Me Gary. Me HUNGRY!' Then he bared his teeth and thumped his chest so hard that Cal thought he'd fall over and die laughing. 'Hey, that reminds me,' Neil said. 'Talking of animals – what's your dad going to do with his panda act? Can I come and see it when it's ready?'

Cal gulped and sat up abruptly. 'No,' he said. What else could he say? Neil looked hurt.

'Why? Aw, man – it's not 'cause I haven't been round in ages, is it?'

'No, no, it's not that.' It was no good, Cal realized: he couldn't go on lying to his best mate. It was time to tell him what was really going on. He sighed. 'Look,' he said, 'I don't expect you to believe me, 'cause I can hardly believe it myself . . .'

'Go on . . .' said Neil, sitting down next to Cal.

'I know what you think you saw,' Cal began. 'Out in the hall, I mean . . .'

'Yeah. Your dad in his panda suit. That's what I'm talking about. So, is there a new act, or not?' Neil asked with a puzzled frown.

'No. There's not,' Cal admitted.

'Eh?' said Neil. 'But you said—'

'I know,' said Cal. 'I lied. That wasn't Dad you saw. Dad's not here . . .' He trailed off. Neil would never believe him if he told him the truth.

Neil was shaking his head. 'I don't get it. So who is that in the panda suit, then?'

'No one,' said Cal. His heart was beating like a drum. He took a deep breath and said in a rush, 'That bear's for *real*! She isn't Dad in a costume, because Dad's gone. He left us yesterday – on my birthday. He and Mum had a row about bacon and he hasn't come back since.'

'Whoa, Cal, that's massive!' Neil's kind brown eyes were wide with shock.

'Yeah,' said Cal sadly. He swallowed, then tried to sound cheerful. 'But it's OK. The panda's going to help. I know how that sounds,' he said quickly, when Neil spluttered in disbelief. 'She's cool, really.

Her name's Pudding. You'll like her when you get a chance to meet her properly.'

'Cal, mate,' said Neil slowly. 'I . . .'

'Honest, it's true!' Cal cried. 'Cross my heart!'

Neil narrowed his eyes. 'And hope to die?' he said.

Cal nodded. 'Yes! Hope to die! *Please* believe me.'

Neil jumped up. 'So let me get this straight: your dad's gone missing. No one knows where he is. And that panda's *real*, and it's come to help you find him?'

'Yes,' said Cal, blushing.

Neil shook his head. 'Nah. You're messing with me,' he said. 'Look – you've gone red.'

'I'm not messing with you! I swear!' Cal protested, leaping to his feet.

Neil narrowed his eyes. 'I'm not that daft,' he said. 'You're Graham Campbell's son – you're the son of a number one prankster! Your dad's put you up to this.'

'Honest, he hasn't,' said Cal. 'Look. I dunno how to prove it to you – you'll just have to take a closer look at her. At Pudding, I mean. There's no zips or buttons or anything on her. Mum's already checked. Pudding is an actual panda. And my dad really has gone,' he finished. He collapsed on to the sofa in a slump with his head in his hands.

Neil chewed his lip. Then he said slowly, 'All right, if you say there's a real, live panda called Pudding staying in your house, then I believe you – you're my best mate. And I'm pretty sure you wouldn't fib about your dad running out on you. So, if you tell me there's a panda here to help out, then . . . well, OK, I guess! But a bear making pancakes with Tabby is not going to get your dad back, is it? So, this calls for an Emergency Meeting,' he said firmly.

He held out his hand and pulled Cal to his feet. Then he marched Cal into the kitchen, where Tabby and Pudding were doing their best to finish up the last of the pancakes while scribbling on sheets of paper strewn across the kitchen table. Luckily for them, Mum was pretty distracted with her phone, and hadn't noticed the mess they were making.

'Ah, boys!' said Mum, looking up. 'Would you like something to eat? There's plenty of pancakes left . . . oh. Well, there are one or two, anyway,' she said, taking the plate away from Tabby. 'I know it's nearly lunchtime, but I'm afraid there's nothing much else in the fridge.'

'No, I'm all right, Mrs C,' said Neil. 'You've got more important things to do.' He eyed the large panda

cautiously.

'If you mean finding Cal's father,' Pudding interrupted, 'then that is exactly what we've been talking about.' She stood up and held a paw out to Neil. 'I'm Pudding the Panda, here to help. I make the impossible possible. I think we may have got off on the wrong foot in the hallway earlier.'

Neil had the good manners to blush – he *had* prodded her in the bottom, after all. 'I'm sorry ... err, Pudding, I thought you were a human in disguise.'

'That's quite all right. It's an easy mistake to make. People rarely see beyond their own noses, after all.'

'Look, Cal!' said Tabby excitedly, jumping up and down on her chair. 'We've been really busy. We've been making posters – see?' She held up a scrappy piece of paper which said, *Hav U Ceen My Dad?* with a badly drawn stick figure of Dad underneath. 'We've been making all sorts of plans to find him.'

Neil looked impressed. 'Sounds good. Cal and I are in the right place, then. I take it this is Kitchen Headquarters,' he said with a wide smile of encouragement.

'Pity you can't spell, Tabs,' said Cal.

Tabby stuck her tongue out at her brother.

'I've already called everyone I can think of,' Mum said, ignoring them both. 'I just wish Graham would answer his phone . . .' She forced a note of brightness into her voice. 'But I'm not going to worry

too much just yet! It hasn't been *that* long, after all. Just a day, which is nothing, really. Is it?'

It didn't sound like nothing. Cal felt his stomach drop. He found himself leaning in towards Pudding, who pulled him close.

'We'll do our best to find him,' the bear soothed. 'That's all anyone can do.'

'Ahem,' said Neil. 'Do I get a hug too?'

Pudding chuckled. 'Huddle up!' she said, beckoning to Neil, Mum and Tabby. 'I'm a bear. There's room for everyone.'

Mum kissed the top of Cal's head as Pudding gave them all a big bear hug. 'Dad will come back when he's ready, sweetheart,' she said softly. 'I'm sure of it. We just had a few cross words, that's all.'

In the silence that followed, the clock on the kitchen wall ticked more loudly than Cal had ever heard it tick before.

'Maybe he just needed some peace and quiet?' Pudding offered. 'Sometimes I like to chew things over after a busy day at the zoo.'

'But Graham hates being alone!' Mum exclaimed. 'He likes people too much to want to be alone for long. I just don't understand . . .' Her chin began to wobble.

Neil coughed. 'Should I go, Mrs C?' he asked. 'I could call my mum to come and get me.'

'No, don't go!' said Cal. He needed Neil now more than ever.

Luckily Mum agreed. 'No, no. Don't mind me, pet.' She dried her eyes and blew her nose loudly as they all took their places again at the table. 'Maybe Pudding's right. Come on, let's think hard about where Graham might have gone to get some peace.'

'You've called a lot of people,' Pudding said. 'But have you actually gone looking for Mr Campbell yourself? When the monkeys play hide and seek in the zoo, they're really cheeky – they always choose a place that's right under your nose, because that's the last place that anyone thinks to look. Hiding in plain sight, my keeper Gerald called it.'

Mum looked doubtful. 'Why would Graham *hide*?

And all night, as well?'

'Have you listened to the news today, Mrs Campbell?' Neil suggested. 'Sometimes you hear stories on the news about people who've gone missing.'

'Oh, no, don't say that!' Mum looked dismayed. 'Do you think something bad has happened?'

'No, no, dear.' Pudding gave Neil her bear-glare. 'I'm sure nothing's happened. But maybe Neil's right – it might be as well to listen, just in case.'

Mum switched on the radio, her face creased with worry.

The news was just starting. Fear fluttered in Cal's chest. What if something terrible had happened to Dad?

'And we have some breaking news . . .' said the newsreader.

Mum glanced at

Pudding. Pudding took hold of Mum's hand. Neil was chewing his lip and Cal couldn't breathe. Tabby, who had run out of paper, carried on drawing on the tabletop beacause no one told her not to.

"...WENT MISSING, We believe, LAST NIGHT..."

the newsreader was saying.

"...door LEFT OPEN and bamboo UNEATEN..."

'Eh?' said Neil. 'Bamboo? That doesn't sound like your dad!'

Cal prodded him to be quiet.

"...possible ANIMAL ESCAPE..."

'Escaped? *Animal?*' Cal repeated.

Pudding started humming loudly. She scraped her chair back and bustled over to the sink.

'Shhh, Pudding!' said Cal. 'Stop humming. They said an animal had escaped . . .' Then a thought occurred to him. 'Pudding?'

"... Was about to be sent to CHINA..."

said the newsreader.

'Pandas come from China,' Neil remarked.

'What's going on?' Tabby said, looking up from her scribbles.

'PUDDING!' Cal cried. 'Have you ESCAPED from the zoo? I thought they'd *sent* you here!'

Crash! A mug fell off the draining board.

'Oops, how very clumsy! I meant to put the kettle

on,' said Pudding, flapping her paws as she turned this way and that. 'Nothing like a nice cup of tea with a spoonful of—'

'SHHHHHH!' said everyone.

"...the **STAR ATTRACTION** of Edinburgh Zoo is a VERY PRECIOUS CREATURE So THE REWARD FOR ANY INFORMATION RELATING TO THE PANDA BEAR WILL BE £500,000—"

'WHAT?' Mum squeaked.

"...and the **ZOO** WILL pay =£3 million= FoR THE **SAFE RETURN** OF THE **BEAST**..."

Tabby, who had been listening very carefully, put down her crayons. Then she took a big breath, opened her mouth and roared: 'NO ONE'S TAKING MY PUDDING AWAY!'

Pudding leant across and turned off the radio with a click. The kitchen went quiet.

Cal was the first to speak. He cleared his throat. 'So, you're a runaway bear. You escaped from the zoo?' he said.

Pudding dipped her head and twiddled her claws.

She rocked on her feet and gave a little nod. 'I – I might have done,' she admitted.

'And they want you back so much that they'll pay a three-million-pound reward?' said Mum. 'That's a lot of money, hen.'

As if anyone needed telling.

Except for Pudding, it seemed. 'How much is three million pounds?' she asked. 'It sounds like a lot of bamboo. Far too much, really,' she said. 'I only need enough to have a full tummy and a sleepy head. Enough is as good as a feast, that's what I always say.'

But Cal was not going to let Pudding change the subject. 'Pudding – are you

really worth *three million pounds?'*

'What a difference that sort of money would make to our lives,' Mum breathed.

'I don't care how much money that is – she's OUR bear!' shouted Tabby.

'Thank you, pet,' said Pudding, giving Tabby a squeeze.

Mum was looking very strange. 'Sweethearts,' she began, 'I should be honest with you about why Dad ran out yesterday. . .' Her face crumpled. 'Lately, Dad's not been making people laugh in the comedy club, and the festival don't want him back. That's a big problem for us – the Edinburgh Festival is where Dad does the most shows, you see. And he's not been paid for months. So you see, some reward money would be a very good thing for us right now.'

'But a very bad thing for Pudding,' said Cal.

Pudding coughed. 'Please don't send me back,'

she said politely. 'I mean, I wouldn't mind going back to the zoo. But I would really rather not go to China. I've lived my whole life here, in Edinburgh. I belong here.'

'But you don't belong to *us*,' said Mum.

There was a bear-sized pause.

'Don't I?' Never had a panda looked more sorrowful.

'Mrs Campbell's right,' said Neil. 'You don't belong to anyone. If anything, you belong in the wild.'

'The Wild?' whispered Pudding. 'What's that? Is it in China?'

'NOT FAIR!' Tabby bellowed. 'Leave Pudding alone.'

'Shut up, Tabby,' said Cal. Someone was going to have to take charge, he felt. They were getting nowhere. 'Mum, I get that we need the money,' he said, 'but you can't seriously be thinking of handing Pudding in if she doesn't want to go?'

Mum was babbling now. 'I know, I know! I don't want Pudding to go either, but what if Dad doesn't come back because we have no money?'

'You can't put a price on Pudding,' said Cal. 'What do you think, Neil?'

'I agree,' Neil said. 'Well, not on *this* Pudding, anyway – a chocolate one, or an apple crumble maybe . . . but a panda should be free.'

Cal gave Mum a meaningful look. 'You see? She's worth more than any reward.'

Mum held up her hands in defeat. 'All right!' she said. 'You're right. You're *all* right. You win! Our panda stays put.'

'Oh, thank you!' Pudding cried.

As everyone cheered and celebrated, Cal's attention was caught by the rattle of the cat flap.

He ran over to the window and peered outside into the fading afternoon light.

A skinny figure was running away from the house. It was clear to Cal who it was, even from behind. *Mike Spiker!* Bully boy – and neighbourhood spy.

Cal's heart sank. Pudding was in deep trouble – and so were the rest of them.

CHAPTER 6

Who Wants to be a Millionaire?

Mike Spiker arrived home shaking with excitement. 'You'll never believe this, Dad! They've got . . . they've got the —'

'Shut up, lad,' his father growled from his armchair, turning up the volume on the TV. 'Can't you see ah'm watchin' the telly?'

'*Pudding is the zoo's Star Attraction . . . any*

information relating to the panda...'

On the TV screen a news reporter stood in front of an empty zoo pen. Next to him was a zoo-keeper with a ginger mous-tache. It was the same story Mike had heard on the radio across the road when he was spying on Cal and his family ... and the panda.

'But that's what I'm trying to tell you, Dad!' Mike hopped up and down like a flea as he pointed at the screen. 'The missing panda! It's at—'

'OOT O' MA WAY!' Spud Spiker yelled, shoving his son to one side.

'*. . . a reward of three million pounds . . .*' the news-reader said.

Mike's father slammed down the drink in his hand and spat out the mouthful he had just swigged.

'YES! And it could all be ours! That's what I'm trying to tell you, Dad!'

Spud Spiker's face turned purple. He stood up. Arms crossed, muscles bulging, he loomed over his son.

'Are . . . you . . . tellin' . . . me . . .' Spud stabbed a sausage of a finger into his son's chest to emphazise each word, 'that YOU know where that panda's at?'

'Yes!' Mike squeaked.

His dad's eyes boggled like a toad's. 'And you've only just this minute thought of comin' to tell me?'

Mike nodded so hard it made him dizzy.

'WELL THEN, WHAT ARE WE WAITING FOR?' Spud shouted. 'Where is it? How do we catch it? Tell me – NOW!' He leant down and picked Mike up by the scruff of the neck. 'Who's got it?'

'Cry-baby Callum Campbell's got it.'

'WHAT YE BLETHERIN' ABOOT?' his dad

roared.

Mike squeezed his eyes shut in fear. 'The panda that's worth three million pounds is in Callum Campbell's house,' he blurted out. 'The Campbells are hiding it!'

He opened one eye cautiously and watched for his dad's reaction. Surely this news would please him? Maybe now his dad would stop calling him a useless waste of space. If he got this right and impressed Spud for once, it might mean no more getting told off by his dad for serving up still-frozen meals. Maybe now – finally – he, Mikey Spiker, would make his dad proud.

Spud Spiker set his son down on the floor with a thud. He bent down and pushed his face right up against Mike's so that his hairy nose squashed Mike's wee one. Then, in a voice so low that Mike had to strain to catch it, his dad said, 'You, ma lad, are a scabby wee liar.'

'No, no, Dad!' Mike said, shaking his head furiously. 'Ah'm no'! I saw it. I did. In their kitchen. Large as life, black and white, and twice as furry. With my own eyes, I saw it!'

'Well, you'll be needin' specs then, laddie,' said Spud. 'An' dinnae think *I'll* be paying for them.' He gave Mike a shove with his foot for good measure. 'Awa' 'n' boil yer heid, ye waste o' space,' he muttered.

'Honest, Dad. I'm telling the truth,' Mike wailed. He knew he was pushing his luck — when his dad turned mean, it was better to leave him be — but this was way too important. 'We've gotta call the zoo, Dad, and tell them. Then we'll get the first half a million quid. Think of all that money. We could finish the rebuilding of this house and sell it at last. An' if we *catch* the panda as well, they'll give us millions of squids more! You heard them just now . . .' He pointed at the telly. 'You could build palaces then.'

Spud Spiker paused to think. If he told his son to shut up, he usually did. So why wouldn't Mike let this stupid story drop? Thinking was not something Spud liked doing. He looked down at his big scarred hands. He preferred using them to his head. He was a builder. He made things. He puffed himself out. He once rebuilt a bothy for Her Majesty the Queen on her Balmoral estate. She had waved at him through the rain. It was his proudest moment. There had not been many since. He glanced around the building site that was

his house. There was so much that needed fixing.

CLUNK...CLICK...WHIRR. The cogs turned and clunked into place in his cement-mixer-like brain once more. If he had that reward money then he wouldn't have to lift a shovel again, he could stop working altogether.

'Well, if you say you're NOT a scabby wee liar, we'd better go see!' Spud said, his eyes glinting. 'And if I find out you ARE telling fibs . . .' He let the thought hang in the air as he dragged Mikey over to their curtain-less front window.

Together they leant forward and peered across the road. The two of them stood side by side as they tried to make out the shapes and shadows moving behind the curtains in the Campbell house. Mike felt a strange warm glow spread through him as his dad put a haggis-sized hand on his shoulder. It was the closest Mike had felt to his dad in . . . well, *for ever*!

'Look!' Mike squealed, as the unmistakeable shape of a big bottom wiggled briefly in the Campbells' window, silhouetted by the light from the front room.

'Well, well, well,' Spud Spiker muttered. 'You know what this means, ma lad?' He laughed and slapped his thigh. 'It's retirement day at last, Mikey boy!'

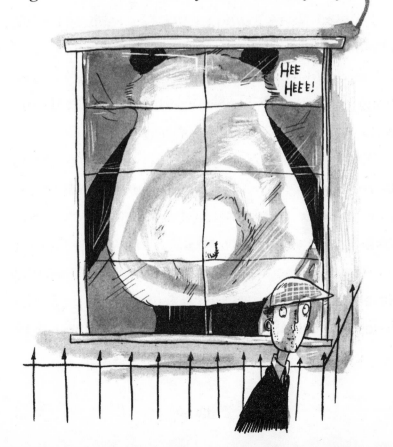

While Mike and his dad were arguing about whether or not there was a panda living across the road, Cal had grabbed Neil and dragged him into the lounge. The two of them needed to talk.

'Where are you two going?' Mum called. 'Now that Pudding is staying, we need to work on getting Dad back!'

'In a minute, Mum!' Cal replied.

'What's up?' Neil asked. He was finding it quite a job keeping up with his pal today.

Cal tugged him to the side of the window, pulled the curtains closed and ducked down behind the sofa. 'Take a look at the house opposite!' he hissed, pointing up at the windowsill.

Neil peered through a chink in the curtains. 'Why are we spying on the Spikers?' he asked.

'Shh!' said Cal, glancing over his shoulder. He

didn't want Pudding coming in and hearing what he was about to say.

'Come on, Cal, tell me – this is getting boring now,' Neil groaned. 'They've got the telly on – big deal. Let's go back and help your mum now – don't you want to find your dad?'

"Course I do – but I'm scared for Pudding too.' Cal nodded over at the Spikers' house, and Neil saw the dark figures of Mike Spiker and his dad lit up by the glow of their TV.

Neil gasped as he finally realized what Cal was trying to tell him. 'Do you think they've heard about the bear on the news?'

'Bound to have done,' Cal replied. 'Their telly's on night and day.'

'But even if they have, they don't know Pudding's *here*, do they?' said Neil, examining Cal's face carefully.

Cal felt his stomach flip. 'That's just it,' he said.

'I heard the cat flap earlier. Then I saw Mike Spiker lurking in our garden, I'm sure of it. He's always spying on me. We're going to have to hide Pudding better from the outside world from now on.'

'Hulllooo?' said a voice behind them. It was Pudding. 'Are you playing hide and seek?'

'Yes,' said Cal. She had given him an idea. 'But not in here,' he added quickly.

Pudding's eyes lit up and she clapped her paws in delight. 'I LOVE a good game. But what's wrong with hiding in here? Those curtains are perfect for me to hide behind.'

'No – no, Pudding,' pleaded Cal as Pudding wriggled behind them. 'You're going to pull them down and then Mum will get cross! Anyway, there are much better places to hide.' He grabbed the panda's paw and pulled her out and into the hall. 'Mum? Tabs?' he called through the kitchen door.

'Come and play hide and seek with us. We need you to count to a hundred while Neil and I go and hide with Pudding.'

'But I want to hide with her!' Tabby complained.

'I know,' said Cal. 'But your turn will come.' He shot Mum a look that said, *Help me!*

Mum played along but her sharp glance at Cal said, *What's up?*

To Tabby, she said smoothly, 'Cal's right, pet. It'll be more fun this way. Come on, Tabs – let's go on a bear hunt!'

'Yay! We're going to catch a BIG one!' Tabby whooped as she covered her eyes and began counting. 'One . . . two . . .'

Cal led Neil and Pudding off to Dad's studio at the back of the house. What had once been the garage was now where Dad kept all the costumes and props for his acts. It was also the best place for

Pudding to be out of sight.

'How *practically perfect*!' the panda exclaimed as she made a beeline for Dad's costume wardrobe. Pudding clambered in and began pulling the costumes around her.

CREEEEEEE-AAAAAAACCCKKK! There was a terrible sound of splintering wood.

'Pudding!' Cal shouted. 'What have you done?'

But the panda was too busy gazing spellbound at the costumes that had come tumbling out. 'I like *this*!' she said, pulling on a wavy grey wig. 'And what about *this*?' she said, picking up a diamond tiara fit for a queen. 'And I have ALWAYS wanted a cloak like *this*!' she added, swooshing an old velvet curtain around her.

'Pudding! Put it all back!' Cal cried. 'We're supposed to be hiding!'

'Ninety-nine . . .' Mum's voice rang out from the

hallway. 'One hundred!'

'Ready or not . . . !' Tabby squealed.

'Quick, we need to put you somewhere else!' Cal cried.

'But Cal,' Neil said quietly. 'Remember what Pudding said about the monkeys at the zoo? Isn't

this hiding in plain sight?' Neil pointed at Pudding, who looked almost unrecognizable in her majestic new outfit.

Tabby and Mum burst into the room before Cal could answer.

'Hey! That's not hiding!' Tabby said, scowling. 'That's dressing up – and making Pudding look silly.' She ran up to the bear and pulled off her wig and the crown, throwing them all on to the floor.

'I thought I looked rather supercalifragilistic—'

BANG! BANG! BANG!

'What on earth is that?' Mum exclaimed. 'Is someone at the door again?'

'It's Dad! It's got to be!' Tabby said excitedly. 'I'll go.'

BANG! BANG! BANG!

'No, no – stop!' cried Mum. 'Dad would never hammer like that.'

'Mum's right,' said Cal. 'I don't think that's Dad.' He put a finger to his lips and looked worriedly at his mother. *Spikers!* he mouthed. He hoped Mum would understand. There had been bad feeling between the Campbells and the Spikers ever since Mike's dad had jeered Cal's off the stage at the comedy club last summer. 'We need to hide Pudding fast. Right now!' he said.

'I think we should all hide together,' said Mum firmly, pulling Tabby close.

'That's not how you play hide and seek,' Tabby protested.

'No, but it's much more fun this way,' said Neil with a wink.

'Find the fun, remember, Tabby?' Pudding took her other hand.

Cal ran into the hall and flicked off the light switch so they were plunged into darkness. Then he tiptoed back to the garage and huddled up with the others. They all held their breath as the thunderous din of banging and thumping on the front door started up again.

'Why can't whoever that is knock politely like anyone else?' Pudding whispered. 'Or use the bell?'

'Because the Spikers are not like anyone else,' Mum murmured.

'Shhhh!' said Cal. 'No talking.'

BANG! BANG! BANG! BANG! BANG! This was followed by the clatter of the letterbox rattling open. 'We know you're in there!' a gruff voice said through the gap.

'Yeah!' a high-pitched voice joined in. 'And we know you've got the bear—'

There was a muffled grunt. 'Dinnae tell the whole street, ye waste o' space!'

'I don't like this game. And I don't want to hide in the dark,' Tabby said in a small voice. 'Why are the Spikers coming to play? We don't like them. Are they going to break the door down, Mum?'

'Tabby's right,' Mum said worriedly. 'I don't know what's going on, but we should find somewhere safer to hide and call the police.'

'What about in the shed?' said Cal. 'We can slip out the back door.'

'But I hate the shed,' Tabby whined.

'So do I,' Cal admitted. 'But right now, I don't think we have a choice.'

They crept down the dark hall, through the kitchen, out of the back door, and down the overgrown

path. 'This really is like going on a bear hunt!' said
Mum, to keep Tabby's spirits up. 'Isn't it, Tabby?'

'No, it's not,' Tabby wailed. 'This is like the bears
are hunting us. And I don't mean Pudding—'

She was interrupted by a horrible groan from the
bottom of the garden.

GEMEOOUUT!

'Whoa! What was that?' Neil gripped Pudding's paw.

'Mum, I don't like it!' Tabby squeaked.

'Shhh!' said Cal, putting his hand over his sister's mouth.

'Do you think it's a g-g-ghost?' whispered Pudding.

'Don't be such dafties,' said Mum, but her voice was shaking. 'It'll be the wind in the trees, that's all.'

Neil shivered. 'It *could* be a ghost. Or a monster. Right now, I'd believe it was anything. I mean, I didn't think there were talking pandas until this morning!'

Pudding hid behind Tabby.

Tabby hid behind Cal.

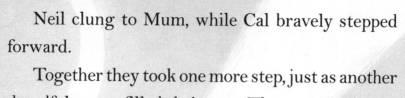

Neil clung to Mum, while Cal bravely stepped forward.

Together they took one more step, just as another dreadful groan filled their ears. There was only one question on everyone's mind . . .

Just what was in that shed?

CHAPTER 7

We're Going on a Dad Hunt

'We'll be all right if we stick together.' Cal sounded braver than he felt. 'There are more of us than there are of – well, of *it*,' he said.

'Wh-what if that's not true?' Pudding whispered. 'What if there are hundreds of "its"?'

Cal swallowed. His throat felt very dry. *Spikers*

behind us and monsters in front of us . . . things are not looking good! He made himself think of Dad. What would Dad say if he was here now? He'd tell him to forget his fears and stand tall. That's what he'd always said about Mike Spiker: *You've got to face up to the bullies, lad.*

He's right, Cal thought. *That is exactly what I have got to do. I've got to be like King Arthur. Or a Marvel Super Hero.*

Mum took Pudding's paw in one hand and Tabby's hand in the other. 'The shed's not that big,' she said reassuringly. 'And it's full of junk. There's no room for hundreds of anything.'

'Unless it's hundreds of monster red ants or killer woodlice,' said Neil.

'Eee—!' Tabby squealed. Mum hugged her close.

They had reached the shed now. Cal made the first move. He gave the door a nervous prod, then leapt back as though he had burnt his fingers. The truth was, he didn't know if he could be as brave as King Arthur after all. What if there were hundreds of monster red ants or killer woodlice inside?

'It's stuck,' he whispered.

'We'll *all* give it a push,' said Neil over his shoulder.

Mum, Pudding and Tabby were hanging back.

'Yes. Come on, we can do this!' Cal said. Just saying it made him feel braver – and it made everyone else feel better too. Mum, Cal and Neil put their shoulders to the door, and then Tabby and Pudding leant in behind them.

No one had quite banked on the force of a one-hundred-kilogram panda pushing behind four humans. Although after what she had done to Dad's costume wardrobe, they probably should have, Cal thought as the door collapsed and they all fell forwards into the shed.

'WHAT IN THE NAME OF THE ROYAL
TATTOO—?' exclaimed a voice from inside.

'Graham?' Mum croaked. 'Is that you?'

'Dad?' Cal whispered, not quite believing his ears.

Pudding picked herself up and everyone got out from under her. 'There! I told you he'd be hiding somewhere that's right under your nose,' said the panda. 'Just like the monkeys hiding in plain sight.'

Cal swung his torch around. Sitting on an old broken toilet next to an open freezer, was a scruffy man who looked as though he had been folded in half. His eyes were ringed with red, his clothes were creased, and in his hand he held a floppy slice of defrosted pizza. His mouth hung open in shock as he stared at Pudding, seeing the giant panda for the first time.

'Dad! It *is* you!' hissed Cal. 'What are you doing in here?'

'Daddy!' yelled Tabby, launching herself into her dad's arms and knocking the pizza straight out of his hand.

'Well, this is weird,' said Neil.

'You're telling me!' said Dad. He leapt up from the loo, banging his head on the ceiling. 'Am I seeing things?'

Cal followed his dad's gaze. 'Oh, sorry, Dad – this is Pudding. Pudding, meet my dad.'

Cal waited for his father to speak, but Mum got in there first.

'Graham, why haven't you answered your phone?' she said. 'We've been worried sick!'

Dad didn't seem to hear her. 'A b-b— What *is* that?' His voice sounded dazed. 'A p-p-p—?'

'It's the panda you got Cal for his birthday, silly!' said Tabby. 'She's come to live with us to be our nanny!'

Dad looked in confusion from Pudding to Mum, then back to Cal. 'Noooo!' he breathed. 'You're pullin' ma chain.'

Neil laughed. 'No, they're not. I thought they were too – I thought the panda was you, Mr Campbell.'

Cal's dad looked doubtful. 'I know I've played a trick or two on you boys in my time,' he said, 'but this isn't fair. I've been locked in here for – what – days? Feels like weeks!'

'It's only been *one* day, Dad. And this is a panda, really it is!' said Tabby.

'Ahem, I am a "she", not an "it", remember?' said Pudding, ruffling Tabby's hair.

Dad's jaw fell open. 'It speaks!' he said, looking around in amusement as if expecting someone to say 'Gotcha!'. When they didn't, his face scrunched into a puzzled frown, 'So it can't be real then, can it?' he said sternly. 'Now, tell me the truth! Where are the zips on this thing? I'll find out who's inside this.' He got up and pinched Pudding on the bum, just like Neil had done.

'Ouch!' Pudding protested. 'I do wish you'd all stop doing that.'

Cal's dad laughed. 'You've got me, Cal,' he said. 'Good one, son! You'll have to take over from me on the stage.'

'Dad,' Cal said, trying to be patient. 'Trust me,

we haven't got time for this now. You'll just have to believe us. The panda is real.'

Pudding nodded. 'It's the truth, Mr Campbell,' she said. 'Delighted to meet you. I am the panda you adopted for Cal's birthday. And – I really can't say this enough – I am a SHE not an IT.'

Cal's da stared at her. He scratched his head. Then he put his hands on his hips and blew out his cheeks. 'So . . . A real-life bear's living here with us?'

'YES!' chorused the others.

'OK! OK!' said Cal's dad, throwing his hands up in surrender. 'It's just that, when I got that present, I thought it was – ye know, a free pass to go to the zoo. I bought it so we could get out more . . . as a family.' He shook his head in bewilderment.

'Oh, Graham,' Mum whispered. 'What a good idea.' In the beam of the torch, Cal could see tears glistening in her eyes. 'What were you thinking, silly-billy, hiding in the shed all this time?'

'I havenae been hiding, hen, I've been trapped!' Dad hung his head. 'The door swung shut on me and I couldnae get it open. I was shoutin' and shoutin' for help – did youse not hear me? I couldnae phone 'cause I dunno where ma phone is – it must still be in the house because I never meant to stay out so long.'

'Listen, Dad, it's brilliant that we've found you – it's all I've been thinking about – but we haven't time to celebrate right now,' said Cal, cutting in. 'We've a bigger problem, Dad. And we need your help. It's the Spikers!'

Hearing the name was enough. Dad put Tabby down and stepped over the remains of the shed. 'Tell me,' he said, a shadow crossing his face.

'They're at the front door,' Cal replied. 'Mike and his dad. Didn't you hear them trying to bang it down? They've come to take Pudding away from us.'

'WHAT?' Dad drew himself up. 'Oh, they have, have they?' He made a face that would have scared even the bravest. 'Well, I'm just about done with Spud Spiker sticking his nose into ma life. Callin' out names when I'm performing my act. Hammering at night when he could be fixing up that house of his during the day. And that son o' his, Mikey, making trouble at school . . . and now they want a piece of you too, do they?' He looked at Pudding – blinked once and then twice – and turned back to Cal. 'We'll see about that!'

And with that, Dad marched down to the back gate. He was a man on a mission, Cal thought proudly. *Just like King Arthur – and I'm right behind you!*

Unfortunately, the Spikers were right in front of them. They had given up on trying to bang the front door down, and had come down the lane at the back of the house. Cal's torch lit up their smirking faces.

'So, where's the bear, you pathetic little weasel?'
Mike said, squaring up to Cal.

'Yeah – swing your torch around and let's
see the black-and-white beastie!' said Spud.

'I'll swing something else around if you're not
careful!' said Cal's dad, stepping out from the shadows and rolling up his sleeves. He was quite a sight
in his unwashed and unshaven state. He looked like

the mighty Scots rugby player he used to be, rather than the down-on-his-luck comedian he had become.

Mike yelped and cowered behind his dad, but Spud stood his ground, ready to put Cal's dad in his place. 'Now you listen to me, Campbell,' Spud growled.

'Er, no. I think it's time you listened to me for once, Spiker,' said Cal's dad. He seemed to grow several centimetres as he spoke. 'What was that you just said, about my son being a weasel?'

Cal glowed. His dad had never stood up to Spud Spiker before. Had something magic happened inside that shed? This was the Dad he remembered, before he got sad and everyone stopped laughing at his jokes.

Spud Spiker took a half step back. With Dad towering over him, he didn't look so scary any more.

'Och, let's talk about this like two grown men,' Spud said, baring a gold tooth in a grin.

Dad made a show of looking around. 'Two grown men, you say? I can only see one right now – and that's me.'

Spud coughed and tried to sound reasonable again. 'I was just – erm – checking up on yer missus,' he said to Cal's dad. 'Making sure she was OK, like. Mikey said you'd gone away for a while.'

'Is that right?' said Dad. 'Well, I'm back now, as you can see.'

'Graham,' Mum's voice rang out anxiously in the

gloom. 'Be careful.'

'Aye, be careful, *Graham*. We know what you've got,' said Spud, recovering his inner meanness. 'And we're not about to let you keep it.'

Dad leant in towards Spud, and Cal felt his knees knock together. Did Dad know what he was doing? And where was Pudding? He couldn't see her or hear her. He hoped she was well out of sight. How were they going to get out of this mess?

Cal kept the torch on the Spikers. That way, he figured, Spud and Mike couldn't see much with the light shining in their eyes.

Just then a kerfuffle broke out behind him and Cal heard Tabby squeak, 'No! Pudding, don't . . . !'

Then an extraordinary figure slid out from the darkness like a queen stepping out of a golden carriage.

'Now what's going on here, young man?' said the

regal figure, pressing a paw to Spud's chest. 'That is not the way to speak to anyone.'

Spud and Mike looked stunned.

Dad gave a snort of laughter, then stopped himself.

Cal gasped. It was Pudding!

She had gone back to get dressed up in Dad's studio, and was draped in the velvet cloak made from a curtain, with the puffed-up wavy grey wig and the diamond tiara on top of her head. She gazed like the Queen at Spud Spiker.

Cal's mouth dropped open. *What is she doing?* he wondered.

'Genius!' Neil whispered to Cal.

Whatever Pudding's plan, it was having a strange effect on Spud. Even in the torchlight, Cal could see that the man's face had gone a dark shade of pink. His jaw hung open, showing every single one of his gold

teeth. His eyes were goggling in their sockets, and he seemed to have lost the power of speech as well.

'Now, my dear man,' Pudding said, dangling a brick-shaped handbag over her arm. 'Why don't you leave these lovely people in peace? You can see that Mr Campbell here has been away from home for a while, and he would like to spend a quiet evening in with his friends and family.'

'I – I – OK,' said Spud, dropping to one knee with his hand on his heart and gazing up at Pudding in an awed manner. It was as though she had cast a spell over him!

'W-who's that woman?' Mike hissed, sidling up to his dad.

'That's a lady, ye numpty. Cannae ye see?' Spud babbled. He bowed his head to Pudding. 'Of course, your – Royalty. Err . . . my Highness,' he said. 'Ah'm dead sorry to be botherin' you on this cold night.

Come on, son,' he said, grabbing Mike by the arm.
'No bears here. Someone else must have it. You heard
Her Majesty, it's time to leave.'

'But Dad...' Mikey whined as he trailed after his
short-sighted father.

Cal turned his torch around on his family and friends as Spud stumbled to his feet and made his way back down the garden with Mikey in tow. In no time, the Spikers had gone.

'Pudding, you were amazing!' he cried.

'That was some act, I have to admit,' said Dad, laughing.

'Queen of Puddings! Who would have guessed.' Neil grinned.

Mum and Tabby threw their arms around the bear. 'You're a star!' they chorused.

'I'll say aye to that!' said Dad. Then, swinging his daughter on to his shoulders, he looked Cal in the eye and said, 'Inside, everyone. Now!'

CHAPTER 8

Money Makes the World Go Round

Cal, Tabby, Mum, Neil and Pudding stood to attention in front of the kitchen counter.

'So, we got rid of them,' said Dad, brushing his hands together.

'For now,' Cal said worriedly.

'Yay!' said Tabby. 'I'm hungry. Is it time for tea now?'

'Oh gosh! I clear forgot about tea!' said Mum.

'Yeah, lunch AND tea,' Tabby grumbled. 'My tummy's rumbling!'

'Och, mine too, pet.' Dad rubbed his stomach. 'I want to know everything that's been going on, but I need to eat something first. Ah'm pure famished!

I dreamt of a fry-up in that shed – a full Scottish!'

'Aw, noooo!' Cal groaned. 'Not bacon!'

'What's wrong with bacon?' Dad asked, frowning.

Cal let out an exasperated huff. 'You *know* what's wrong with it – you and Mum are always arguing about it. You were even arguing about it on my birthday!'

Dad mouthed *Bacon?* at Mum, who pulled a face and shrugged.

'Mum said you hadn't brought home any bacon,' said Cal. He felt upset just thinking about it.

Then Dad's mouth began to twitch. The twitch turned into a full-blown grin, and he threw back his head and roared with laughter. 'Bacon!' he squeaked. Then Mum seemed to get the same joke, and soon she was giggling too.

'What's so funny?' said Pudding. She pulled off her wig and tiara and picked up her flowerpot hat, wedging it firmly back on to her head, and gave Dad and Mum a stern Mary-Poppins-style glare. 'Grownups should *never* laugh at children, it's neither fair nor kind.'

'They're not being mean, Pudding,' said Neil. 'It's just what all parents do. You'd think they'd have learnt not to, from when *they* were children, but they never seem to.'

'Dad!' Cal protested. 'Mum!'

'What's so funny?' Tabby glared at her parents,

copying Pudding.

His parents pulled themselves together. 'Sorry,' they said, biting the insides of their cheeks to stop themselves from laughing.

Dad crouched down and put his arms around Tabby and Cal. 'We weren't arguing about bacon, kids,' he explained. 'Not exactly — we had had some cross words over money, that's all. I'm sorry that we made you worry.'

'But — what's money got to do with bacon?' Tabby asked. 'Has the supermarket run out of bacon?'

Mum smiled. 'It's just an expression. *Bringing home the bacon* means earning money,' she said. 'We didn't want

to upset you, so we used it as a kind of code . . .'

Cal rolled his eyes. Why did adults have to make everything so complicated?

Pudding cleared her throat. 'Ahem. I – I could make your bacon problem go away,' she said quietly. 'If I hand myself in at the zoo,' she went on, 'you could still collect the reward money. Then you can have bacon for breakfast, lunch and tea.'

Tabby gave a whimper. Cal felt a cold shiver run through him.

Mum clasped one of Pudding's big paws in both her hands. 'We can't let you do that, hen,' she said. 'Can we, Graham?'

Dad stood up and ran a hand through his hair. 'Reward money?' he said, looking confused.

'What reward money?'

'The reward money from the zoo—' Pudding began.

'But Mum!' said Tabby, looking at Mum in horror. 'You said she could stay!'

'Now, wait a minute,' Dad said, holding up his hands. 'Why does the zoo want to offer a reward? I adopted the bear for Cal!'

Cal took a deep breath and, ignoring his sister's protests, he told his Dad about his email to Pudding, and all about how she had escaped to come and help him, finishing with the news story.

'Phew!'

Dad gave a long, low whistle. 'So, this reward – how much are talking about?' he asked.

'Now, Dad,' said Cal, looking alarmed. 'You can't be thinking of returning her?'

'NO!' Tabby burst into noisy tears. 'Please, can we keep her? The zoo wants to send her to China. And she doesn't want to go.'

'I don't,' Pudding agreed, shaking her head sadly.

'Don't do it, Dad!' Cal implored. 'Who cares if she's worth three million pounds—'

'*Three million pounds?*' Dad yelped.

'SHHHHHHH!' Mum looked around her. 'They'll hear you across the road!'

Dad's face was a picture as he put two and two together and came up with three million. 'So THAT'S why that bodger of a builder, Spud Spiker was so keen to get his mitts on her!' he growled. He paused and looked at the expressions on the faces of those he loved. 'Neil,' he said, turning to Cal's friend for support. 'You're a sensible wee man. Aside from the money, can ye no' see that this panda belongs in the zoo? We'd be breaking the law to keep her here—'

'No,' said Neil, looking fierce. 'Everyone was sad before Pudding came along. She's made everything better since she got here. And she wants to be here. It's her free choice.'

'Neil's right,' said Mum, stepping in. 'It was you that left, Graham. I had to make a decision to let the bear stay in our home. You walked out of that door and we didn't know where you'd gone, or if you'd be coming back. We know now it was all a mistake, and we're glad that you're here –' she reached out and squeezed his hand – 'but the fact is, Pudding is one of the family now. Our family. She's shown us what's important, and she's brought fun and laughter back into our home. And, don't forget,' she added, 'adopting this panda was your idea. So you can't just send her back.'

'I see,' Dad said, sitting down hard. He rubbed his hand over his tired face. 'OK, then. Pudding can stay. But how are we going to keep her safe? And what are we going to do about the money we need?' He sighed heavily.

Then his eyes fell on the wig and tiara that Pudding had left on the kitchen table.

'Aha!' he said slowly. 'Now, that gives me an idea!'

AHA!

NOW THAT
giVES me
an IDEA!

CHAPTER 9

BAMBOOzled!

'Well, don't keep us in suspense!' Cal urged Dad. 'What's your big idea?'

Dad paced the kitchen. 'I've been thinking for a while that I need a new show,' he said. 'And a comedy partner as well. So . . .' He sat down at the table and pointed at Pudding. 'How about you join me, Pud?'

Pudding looked delighted. She danced over to the back door and picked up Mum's umbrella, striking a pose that Mary Poppins would have been proud of. 'Well!' she said, 'I was the Star Attraction at the zoo, and I always got lots of lovely laughs from the children . . .'

'We could call it the *P and Dad Show*,' said Dad, warming to his idea. 'Get it? I could tell bear-y bad jokes . . . it would be a sell-out! Ticket PANDAmonium!'

'Seriously, Graham?' Mum asked, raising an eyebrow.

Tabby clapped her hands with glee. 'The P and Dad Show!' she said. 'I want to see it!'

Cal coughed loudly. 'Ahem! There's just one problem with that, Dad,' he said. 'Right now, Pudding is a Most Wanted Panda, and the minute she goes on stage with you, she'll be as good as caught.'

'Cal's right,' said Mum.

'You could be arrested for panda-napping,' Neil pointed out.

Dad pulled a disappointed face.

'I have another suggestion,' Cal chipped in. 'If we can fool everyone into thinking that Pudding is no longer on the loose and safe in China, then after the fuss has died down, you could still perform together – no one will suspect she's *that* panda. People soon forget. It's hiding in plain sight, like you said about the monkeys, Pudding – right? They'll just think she's a person dressed up in a panda suit – there's plenty of people in costume around the city during the festival.'

'That's true!' Mum agreed. 'Edinburgh is chock-a-block with people in fancy dress at festival time. A panda wouldn't surprise anyone.'

Neil looked less sure. 'Yes, but how can we make

the zoo believe that she's got to China?'

'We could ask this?' said Pudding, holding up the paw on which she was still wearing Gerald's lost watch. 'It belonged to my keeper, Gerald,' she explained. 'I think he dropped it. That's how I received your message, Cal. And how I sent one to you too, Neil,' she added.

'Let me look at that,' said Dad. He reached over and examined it closely. 'My, that's fancy,' he said. 'Yes, look – it has a tiny inbuilt robot. You can ask

it anything. Hey, Sid!' he called to the watch.

Nothing happened.

'Let me try more politely,' said Pudding.

'Good afternoon, Gerald's watch?'

The watch suddenly sprang to life. 'What can I help you with?' it asked.

Dad grinned. 'Isn't it clever?'

'Try asking it how we can make people believe that a panda has gone back to China, Dad!' Cal said.

A list of search results immediately pinged up on the screen:

How to transport a panda

How to feed a panda

Pandas in China

Panda returns to China

Pudding clicked on the first link, and a tiny video came up of a panda in a crate on an aeroplane. The panda was chewing on a bamboo shoot as a voiceover said, '*This is Bei-Bei. He was flown from Washington DC to Chengdu in China in a crate . . .*'

Pudding shut it down quickly. 'I don't like the

look of that,' she whispered.

'But that's it!' Cal shouted, punching the air as an idea occurred to him. 'We film you!'

'Me?' said Pudding.

'Yes!' said Cal. 'We can make a video, upload it to YouTube using your watch, or I can use my tablet – a video that will show the world you've made it to China. No one will wonder how you got there – they'll just be glad that you *did*.'

Neil frowned. 'But China doesn't look much like Edinburgh . . . how will we make it look real?'

'Ask the watch what China looks like!'

'Good thinking, Tabby,' Pudding said. 'Hello again, Gerald's watch – could you please show me pictures of pandas living in China?'

PING!

This time loads of images popped up, of black-and-white bears sitting in leafy bamboo groves on chilly-looking Chinese mountainsides.

'Not so different to Edinburgh then – cold, damp and hilly!' Dad said with a grin.

'Except we don't have any bamboo,' Cal pointed out.

'But you do have *this*!' Pudding said, pointing at the large spindly houseplant in the corner of the room.

Neil's eyes lit up. 'Genius!'

Pudding broke off a long stalk from the plant. 'And it looks delicious,' she added. 'Why have I not noticed it before?' She popped the end of the stalk in her mouth.

'Hey!' said Mum. 'You've already ruined my winter pansies.'

Cal was on a roll. 'Now, Pudding, go and stand in front of the plant and pretend to chew it while

I grab the tablet.'

Pudding did as she was told while Cal rushed upstairs and was down again in a jiffy.

'OK, Pud – start munching. And . . . action!' He pressed the 'record' button.

'PAN-da the camera to the left!' Dad called out.

'Quiet, Dad – no panda puns!' Cal hissed.

Pudding put on a great performance, strolling around the plant and making panda eyes for the

camera. The Star Attraction of Edinburgh Zoo was
putting on the show of her life!

'And . . . cut!' Cal said at last, pressing the 'stop' button. 'That was great, Pudding. I think it will work.'

'Ugh,' said Pudding, spitting out the last leaf. 'I'm glad I don't have to eat this stuff for real. It doesn't taste as good as it looks.'

'Thank goodness for that!' said Mum.

Dad clapped Cal on the shoulder. 'Brilliant work, lad. Now upload it to YouTube. Time to BAMBOOzle the world!'

CHAPTER 10

Panda-ly Perfect in Every Way

In the days that followed, the news was all over town.

'You think my puns are bad,' Dad said, shaking out the paper. 'They're nowhere near as lame as these!'

'Och, I'm not so sure about that,' said Mum, teasing.

'Well, our "news" is out there now – in *black and white*! Get it?' Cal laughed.

'Fake news. You are one smart lad,' said Dad, tweaking his son's chin.

'I'm so terribly sorry about the bacon, everyone,' said Pudding, coming to the table with a mound of burnt-looking stuff. 'I can't seem to get the hang of cooking very well. Perhaps you won't be having it for breakfast, lunch and tea ever.'

'Don't you worry about that, Pudding,' said Mum, patting the seat next to her. 'We're just happy to have you here with us, safe and sound.'

'Yes, we are!' said Tabby. She climbed into Pudding's lap and curled up like a kitten.

'It's so very kind of you to let me stay,' said Pudding. 'And I love my new shed. It won't be long before I can lie on the roof in the shade of my very own bamboo grove, hidden from nosy neighbours!'

'You're welcome, Pud,' said Dad. 'And you're not to worry about the reward money, because I've got even bigger plans for our new show.'

'Really?' said Mum, shooting a doubtful glance at Cal, who said, 'Are you sure it's safe to show Pudding off to audiences just yet, Dad?'

'They won't know what they're seeing,' said Dad. 'I've worked it all out. It's probably best if you don't have a speaking part in the show,' he explained to Pudding. 'So you'll only be miming. But listen – bet you can't guess what the new show's going to be called? I've come up with a new name. It's pure dead brilliant!'

'Och, Graham, not another terrible panda joke?' said Mum.

'Tell us, Dad!' said Tabby.

'It is a pun, as it happens,' Dad was grinning fit to burst. 'One o' my best!'

Cal wracked his brain, running through all the puns his dad might come up with. It was going to have be a really good one.

Dad was watching Cal trying to figure it out. 'Come on, Cal,' he said, with a glint in his eye. 'It's a family show . . . it doesn't matter if the jokes are silly . . .' He hinted, 'It stars a dressed-up bear who mimes, and it's something people go to see at Christmas!'

'Dad . . .' Cal said, smiling as the penny dropped. 'You're not putting on a PANDA-MIME?'

'Got it in one!' said Dad.

'Oh, no, you're not,' said Mum.

'Oh, yes, I am!' said Dad. He looked proud as punch as Mum hugged him.

'I love it!' Pudding exclaimed. 'How about we put on *PANDArella*?' she said, giving a twirl. 'I can wear my tiara. Or *Panda in Boots*? Or *Peter PANda*?' She

giggled. 'It doesn't matter – whatever it is, it'll be my BEST,' she raised a paw above her head, 'my most EXCITING,' she turned her feet to three o'clock, 'most WONDERFUL,' she looked skywards and hitched up an imaginary skirt, 'Panda Show EVER! It will be . . .' She paused and looked expectantly at her new-found family.

Mum and Dad looked at Cal who looked at Tabby, and they all laughed as they finished Pudding's sentence.

'. . . practically perfect in every way!'

The End!

Acknowledgments

I will never forget the experience of making a book about a panda. There are many people to thank.

Firstly, to publishers Rachel Hickman, Barry Cunningham and the team at Chicken House. Thank you for keeping the faith and bearing with me. Also enormous thanks to Anna Wilson, who graciously knocked my mad story ideas into a wonderful Pudding-shaped story. Thanks to the originator Vikki Anderson via the Big Idea for the fantastic concept that acted as a springboard into much more . . .

Special thanks to Jodie Hodges and Emily Talbot, my agents at UA. I appreciate all you do, often quietly and behind the scenes, on my behalf.

Making a book about a panda has taken me to many places: to Edinburgh Zoo, to see the delightful real pandas (I fell in love with them at first sight). It took me to Cornwall with dear friend, studio-mate and photojournalist Hazel Thompson on writing weeks away from the studio. Here, we blasted away the cobwebs on a blustery Fistral Beach, and said 'Hello' to almost every dog in Cornwall. Thank you for helping to open up those wide imaginative spaces in our brainstorming sessions, for your depth, and for buying the coffee/cider. Here's to more . . .

The book later took me to Plymouth in the Spring of 2020, where I spent three months of a nationwide lockdown illustrating *Panda at the Door* surrounded by Lego in my niece's bedroom. Thank you Iris for allowing me to use your bedroom as a studio; it was the perfect refuge during a very strange time. You will always be a delight and joy to me.

Enormous thanks to the rest of my family – Roger, my father, for your steadfastness, your wisdom and your delightful eccentricity. My brother Oliver, your quick wit, strength and perseverance is completely inspirational. To Jess, my sister-in-law, you are one of the kindest people I know . . . and thanks to my fellow red-headed niece Rosie for being the joy that you are.

To great friends Sarah Ajayi, Yvonne Gill, Shunu Pellow, Paul and Sue Hanbury, Ben and Ruth for all your encouragements, hilarity and support over the years. Thank you.

Finally, this book is dedicated to my mother Diana, who passed away suddenly in 2015. I am so grateful for all the fun, her enormous heart, her joyful humour, and general silly shenanigans. I would not be doing what I do without her – let's call it legacy.

MILTON THE MIGHTY by EMMA READ
Illustrated by ALEX G GRIFFITHS

When spider Milton discovers he's been branded deadly, he fears for his life and his species. Alongside his buddies, big hairy Ralph and daddy-long-legs Audrey, he decides to clear his name. But to succeed, Milton must befriend his house human, Zoe. Is Milton mighty enough to achieve the impossible?

'. . . a charming and thoughtful read.'
THE SCOTSMAN

Paperback, ISBN 978-1-911490-81-4, £6.99 • ebook, ISBN 978-1-912626-31-1, £6.99

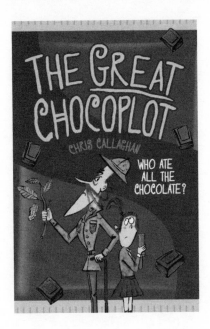

THE GREAT CHOCOPLOT by CHRIS CALLAGHAN

It's the end of chocolate – for good! A chocolate mystery . . . At least that's what they're saying on TV. Jelly and her gran are gobsmacked – they love a Blocka Choca bar or two. But then a train of clues leads back to a posh chocolate shop in town owned by the distinctly bitter Garibaldi Chocolati. Is it really the chocopocalypse, or a chocoplot to be cracked?

'With an excellent cast of characters, laugh-out-loud
moments, and witty and sharp observations, this
is a great choice for fans of Dahl and Walliams.'
THE GUARDIAN

Paperback, ISBN 978-1-910002-51-3, £6.99 • ebook, ISBN 978 -1-910655-57-3, £6.99

GRANNY MAGIC by ELKA EVALDS
Illustrated by TEEMU JUHANI

Will's beloved granny made cakes and knitted itchy jumpers – that's what he thought. But when she passes away and dodgy Jasper Fitchet moves in to their village, dark magic begins to unravel in Knittington. Can Will and his gran's old craft group tie Fitchet in knots? With the help of her old motorbike and a flock of magical sheep, they might just do it . . . so long as they don't drop a stitch.

'This joyous celebration of spinning and spells features motorbike stunts and gold-fleeced sheep.'
THE GUARDIAN

Paperback, ISBN 978-1-912626-19-9, £6.99 • ebook, ISBN 978-1-912626-65-6, £6.99